SCARY

STORIES

tanya
SAVORY

 THE TOWNSEND LIBRARY

SCARY STORIES

TP THE TOWNSEND LIBRARY

For more titles in the Townsend Library,
visit our website: **www.townsendpress.com**

Copyright © 2015 by Townsend Press, Inc.
Printed in the United States of America

9 8 7 6 5 4 3 2 1

Illustrations © 2015 by Hal Taylor

Townsend Press, Inc.
439 Kelley Drive
West Berlin, NJ 08091
permissions@townsendpress.com

ISBN-13: 978-1-59194-457-7

Library of Congress Control Number:
2014954352

CONTENTS

A Night in the Woods

Three friends were sitting around a crackling fire in a remote campground far back in the Maine woods. Overhead, a full yellow moon hung, shedding a warm light on the dark forest. The boys had just graduated from high school three months earlier, and they were enjoying one last trip to their favorite park before heading off to different colleges.

"Where *is* everyone?" Cooper asked as he poked the fire. "Usually, this campground is packed in August."

"I guess Randall scared everyone away," Manuel said with a snort.

"Yeah," Rob agreed. "Everyone watch out for make-believe monsters roaming the Maine woods!" All three boys laughed and shook their heads.

Only two other fires glimmered farther down the dirt road in the campground. One of the fires belonged to an old man named Randall, who had stopped by the boys' campsite earlier to warn them about a crazy dog that was on the loose somewhere back in the woods.

"Word around these parts is that that dog is as big as a bear and twice as mean," old Randall had said to the boys. "It can bite your arms and legs off with one snap. And what's more, it can run faster than a car. And some people even say it can fly."

The three friends had looked at each other quickly, suppressing their laughter.

"We'll definitely keep an eye out for it," Cooper had said politely. "Thanks for the warning."

After that, Randall had wandered down to the only other camper, a tall man in a black t-shirt and heavy black boots, and appeared to be warning him, too. The tall man listened for less than a minute and then shook his head. When Randall persisted, the tall man seemed to lose his patience.

"You're the crazy one," the man had finally said in a loud, irritated voice. "Why don't you just mind your own business, you loony, and stop bugging people!"

Cooper, Rob, and Manuel had a few more laughs about it as they watched their campfire slowly burn itself out. The night grew unusually chilly for late August, and a far-off wind whispered through the trees. In spite of the fact that Rob had laughed the most at the idea of a giant flying dog, he now shivered and strained his eyes in the darkness to look for anything suspicious around the campground. The other campfires were nothing but dim, glowing coals, and the surrounding woods were deathly quiet. But Rob thought he could see the outline of the tall man leaning against a tree. Was he watching for the dog?

"I'm beat," Manuel yawned.

"Me too," Cooper agreed, echoing Manuel's yawn. "Who's taking first guard watch for the dog?"

In joking response, Manuel whistled sharply and said, "Come here, boy! Dinner's ready! Fresh arms and legs!"

All three boys laughed as they crawled inside their tent and into their sleeping bags. But long after Manuel and Cooper had begun snoring, Rob lay awake listening. The distant whispering wind slowly seemed to rise to a howl. Was that a real howl or just the wind? Rob's heart began beating faster.

This is ridiculous, he thought as he forced his eyes to close. *I'm 18 . . . not some little kid who believes in fairy tales.*

But at that very moment, a shrill scream ripped through the campground's quiet. Rob sat bolt upright, his heart racing.

"Wh-what was *that*?" he gasped as he shook Manuel and Cooper awake. "Did you hear that? Someone screamed!"

"Dude, chill," Cooper said sleepily.

"Just a screech owl," Manuel mumbled. "Sounds like a scream, but . . . um . . ." Manuel had already fallen back to sleep. Cooper had never really woken up.

Rob remained sitting up. That had definitely not been an owl. And now a new eerie sound drifted across the campground.

Draaaaag . . . draaaag . . .

And then, very clearly, another scream followed by a desperate "HELP!" echoed down the dirt road not far from the other two campsites. This time, both Cooper and Manuel jerked awake and then bolted upright in their sleeping bags.

"What the . . ." Cooper whispered.

"Okay, screech owls don't scream for help," Manuel said breathlessly.

"Shhh," Rob said. "Listen . . . there's something else."

Draaaaag . . . draaaag . . .

"What is that sound?" Cooper asked shakily. "Whatever's making it is getting closer."

Draaaag . . . draaag . . .

All three boys were silent for a moment, holding their breath and listening. The dragging sound had stopped, and the only sound was the soft rustling of a light breeze through the trees and an occasional pop from the dying embers of their fire. The crickets had all stopped chirping after the screams, but now they resumed their carefree midnight lullaby.

"Maybe crazy old Randall just had a nightmare," Manuel suggested.

"Yeah. Everything seems to be okay now," Cooper agreed.

Rob didn't say anything for a minute. Finally he sighed and said, "Well, whatever that was, it doesn't seem to be—"

GROOOWWWLLLL!!!!!

A hideous, deep growling and snarling was coming from just across the road. It was unlike any animal or human sound the boys had ever heard. In an instant, all the crickets hushed. The growl was followed by a high-pitched, hair-raising howl that echoed through the forest.

"Oh, man!" Rob shouted in terror. "The dog! We've gotta get out of here right NOW!"

In a confusion of untangling sleeping bags, grasping blindly for keys, and scrambling out of the tent, the three boys dashed for Cooper's pickup truck. It was parked close to the tent, but to Rob, it didn't seem nearly close enough. In the fading moonlight, Rob gasped at the sight he saw when he dared to look in the direction of the howl. A huge creature stood on its hind legs not twenty yards away. The darkness hid the creature's face, but its long arms were raised over its head, and its sharp claws were silhouetted against the moon.

The boys piled into the truck's cab and slammed and locked the doors. Gravel sprayed and tires squealed as they roared down the dirt road and out of the campground.

"Did you *see* that thing?" Rob asked in a shaking voice. "That was no dog!"

"Was it a grizzly?" Manuel asked when he'd finally caught his breath. "There are some grizzlies that come down from the mountains sometimes looking for food."

"No way," Rob said. "It had long legs like . . . like a wolf, but it was standing upright. I don't get it."

"The only thing we need to get right now is out of here," Cooper said as he focused on the road. "The closest town is ten miles away. We gotta get there and get help for whoever screamed."

All three boys were quiet for several minutes. Rob wondered if the creature had attacked old Randall, the tall man, or both. More than that, he wondered if whoever was attacked was still alive. He doubted it.

"What's the problem, Coop?" Manuel suddenly asked. "Why are you slowing down?"

"I've got the gas pedal all the way to the floor!" Cooper said nervously. "Something's wrong."

"What do you mean something's *wrong*?" Rob asked in a strained voice. "We can't break down! We're still miles from that town, and if that thing . . ."

Clunk!

In a jerking motion, the truck shuddered and thumped against the road as if something was trying to pull it backward. Manuel and Rob spun around at the same time to look out the back window.

"N-no way," Rob gasped. In a split second,

he felt his mouth go dry, and a rush of cold terror flowed through him. He rubbed his eyes and looked again.

"This can't be happening," Manuel said in a low, terrified voice. "Are we seeing things?"

Running behind their truck was the creature. With one huge paw grasping the truck's tailgate, it was pulling at the truck and trying to make it stop. Now, in the red glow of the taillights, the creature's face was visible. Rob was horrified to see the long snout of a wolf, a lolling tongue, and rows of sharp, glistening teeth.

"Slam on your brakes, and see if you can throw it off some way," Manuel said desperately to Cooper, who was staring into the rearview mirror with wide eyes.

But now the wolf creature had crawled into the bed of the truck. It crouched low, peering into the cab with glowing yellow eyes. For a split second, Rob locked eyes with the monster. There was something about it that seemed almost humanlike in the way it sized up the window and then grinned. Suddenly, the creature pressed both of its huge paws against the window and howled. Then, with a mighty blow, it smashed the cab window. Glass flew everywhere, and the chilly night air blew in, along with the rank, deadly smell of the creature.

"NO!" all three boys screamed. Cooper swerved the truck wildly from side to side and then slammed on the brakes. With a howl of anger, the wolf creature tumbled off and into the weeds beside the road.

"Go! Go!" Rob and Manuel both shouted at once to Cooper. In a roar, the pickup took off again along the dirt road through the forest. But the monster, already on its feet and running, was quickly gaining ground. Closer and closer it came until Rob could see its yellow eyes blazing just behind them. It seemed to grin wickedly and then . . .

"It's back! How did it . . . ? Oh, *no*!" the boys yelled.

With a giant leap that sent the monster completely airborne for several seconds, the creature landed with a heavy thud in the bed of the truck. Cooper did his best to throw the beast out of the truck bed with sharp swerves, but this time the creature held on. Suddenly, through the broken window, it reached wildly for Rob and Manuel. Rob could feel the hot breath of the wolf creature on his shoulder, and sharp claws raked his arm. Rob squirmed and struggled, but the cab of the truck was too small to avoid the wolf's reach.

Just as the wolf fixed a painful grip on Rob's arm, Manuel grabbed a soda bottle that had been rolling around on the floor and slammed it down on the wolf's snout, shattering the bottle. The creature howled, released its grip on Rob, and tumbled backwards. But now it was terribly angry. After regaining its balance, the wolf reached through the window with both paws and grabbed Manuel around the neck, snarling and snapping.

"Do something!" Manuel managed to choke out. "Anything!"

Cooper zigzagged hard to the left and right of the road, but the beast's hold on Manuel kept it steady. Now the wolf opened its mouth wide and leaned in toward Manuel's neck. Slobber drooled on Rob's shoulder as Rob, in sheer panic, looked around the truck cab for any kind of weapon. In desperation, Rob picked up a shard of glass from the broken bottle. Blindly, he slashed in the direction of the wolf's mouth. A spray of blood whipped across Rob's face as the wolf jerked its head and yelped painfully.

Part of the beast's tongue had been cut off, and the second the wolf saw its own blood, it retreated to the back corner of the truck bed. It shuddered violently and then . . .

"What on earth . . . how . . . ?" Cooper sputtered as he slowed down and gawked at what he saw in the rearview mirror.

All three boys watched with disbelief as the huge wolf shrank down into the form of a man dressed in dark, ragged clothes. The man hunched over and held his head in his hands for several seconds. Then he winced at the pain in his mouth, glared with glowing yellow eyes at the boys, and leaped from the truck. Within moments, he had vanished into the dark forest.

"No way," Rob barely whispered. "That was a . . ."

Rob was too afraid and in too much disbelief to finish his sentence. There was a long silence as the boys tried to catch their breath and comprehend what they had just seen. Was it possible?

"A werewolf," Manuel finally said as he rubbed his neck. "He turned back into a man when he saw his own blood!"

Cooper just stared into the woods and shuddered.

An hour or so later, as the sun was coming up, the boys returned to the campground with two police officers and an ambulance for either Randall or the tall man—or both. The boys agreed to keep the whole werewolf thing a secret. They knew no one would believe them. They simply explained that they had been chased by what seemed to be a huge rabid wolf.

"Keep clear!"

As the police and the boys pulled into the campground, paramedics were already loading someone into the ambulance. A large puddle of blood shimmered in the morning sun.

"Don't know if this old guy is going to make it, but he's still alive," one of the paramedics said to the police officer. "One of his legs is half gone, and the other one is pretty mangled. It looks like he was trying to drag himself to where the boys were camping."

Rob suddenly felt sick. That dragging sound—now it made sense. He and the other two boys just stared at each other and shook their heads.

"Poor Randall," Cooper whispered. "He was right!"

The boys looked toward the tall man's campsite, where one of the police officers was leaning over a picnic table, looking down at the tall man, who just sat there nodding. After several minutes, the officer returned and shrugged at the other officer.

"Says he was in town eating when everything happened, and when he returned, he just went to sleep. Never saw that old guy in the road."

The other officer scratched his head. "I'll go talk to him, too."

"Well, you can talk all you want, but he has to write everything down," the officer said. "He had some kind of accident recently, and his tongue was cut pretty badly."

A prickly shot of horror coursed through Rob. He glanced at Cooper and Manuel, and then all three boys turned together slowly to look at the tall man. He stood up from the picnic table and faced them. He folded his long arms.

A broad, evil grin spread across his face, and his eyes flashed with a sickly yellow glow.

■ ■ ■

On Pins and Needles

"**H**old up there, little dude!"

Andre jumped and whipped his head around, peering into the dark alley beside the empty street. Who had said that? He couldn't see anyone. Andre reached his hand into his pocket and protectively grabbed the $72 he had earned. Then he kept on walking at a quicker pace.

"You got a hearing problem, bro?"

Andre felt a strong hand grasp his arm and yank him backwards. Facing him were three older boys from his high school. The biggest one, Reggie, had just been expelled for fighting last week. Word had gotten around school that he'd had a knife and had even threatened a teacher. Now Reggie folded his muscular arms and sneered at Andre.

"Where are you going in such a big hurry?"

Andre looked from Reggie to the other two boys, Steve and Willie. Andre knew that all three boys were in a gang and that they always got whatever they wanted—or else. Their specialty was beating up younger kids and stealing money or belongings from them. Andre shoved his hand down into his pocket and gripped his money tighter. Then he just shrugged his shoulders.

Whup!

A stinging backhanded slap from Reggie nearly knocked Andre over.

"Man, you better speak up when we talk to you!" Reggie shouted. "I asked you where you were going."

Andre looked from face to face. He knew he was in trouble, no matter what he said or did.

"I'm just going home," Andre said, nodding down the street. "I live right up there."

The truth was that Andre was still two blocks from his grandmother's apartment in downtown New Orleans. He'd taken a part-time job stocking shelves in a corner grocery store to help out at home with bills and to have a little spending money for himself. Tonight he had cashed his first paycheck at the store before heading home. He was looking forward to giving his grandma half the cash.

"Whatcha got in your pocket?" Steve asked with a grin. "Looks like you're guarding something. We probably need to see what you're hiding from us before we let you go."

Reggie still had a tight grip on Andre's arm, and now he squeezed tighter.

"Nothing," Andre said nervously. He pulled his hands out of his pockets and opened them up innocently.

In a flash, the three boys slammed Andre to the ground. Willie pulled Andre's arms over his head in a painful lock while Steve put a heavy foot on Andre's chest.

"Yeah, this don't look like 'nothing' to me!" Reggie crowed as he pulled the cash out of Andre's pocket.

"That's mine!" Andre said angrily.

"Not anymore, loser," Reggie shouted. "And since you lied to us, you're gonna get it now."

With that, Steve gave Andre a sharp kick in the ribs while the other two boys punched Andre. Andre protected himself as well as he could by curling into a ball, but he could already feel his lip swelling and his nose bleeding. Finally, the blows stopped.

"Unless you want more of the same," Andre barked, "you better have some more cash for us tomorrow night. And don't even try ratting on us or not showing up. You gonna be in serious trouble if we don't see you here, same time. You got that?"

"Got it," Andre wheezed.

Andre limped out of the alley, his mind in a haze of pain and fear. Where was he going to get more money in just 24 hours? And what was Grandma going to say about his busted lip and bloody nose? He reached into his empty pocket, and tears stung his eyes.

"It's not fair!" Andre said out loud to himself in frustration.

"No, it isn't, is it?" said a crackly voice from behind him.

Andre whirled around with his fists clenched and raised. But it was just an old hunched-over woman with a brightly colored turban wrapped around her head. She carried a tattered black bag in one hand and a knotty walking stick in the other. The top of the stick had a small skull on it. It looked as if the skull was grinning at Andre.

"I—I'm sorry," Andre apologized. "I didn't hear you coming up behind me." How *had* she just suddenly appeared? Andre glanced around nervously.

"Something needs to be done about those three bullies," the old woman said with a strange smile. Two gold teeth shimmered in the streetlight. "Don't you agree?"

"What?" Andre asked, confused. He noticed the old woman smelled vaguely of chocolate and cinnamon. It was weird and comforting at the same time.

"Oh, I've seen them making trouble for some time now," the woman continued. "I can see them from my balcony."

Andre looked up to where the old woman pointed. A worn iron balcony looked directly down on the alley where the boys had been. A candle flickered on a small table, and an odd reddish glow came from the window behind the balcony. The outline of a black cat was framed in the window. Even though the night was warm, Andre felt a prickly chill creep through him.

"So tell me, Andre," the old woman said as she crept very close. "Wouldn't you say that the time has come for those three boys to learn a lesson?"

She laid her hand on Andre's arm, and an electric sensation buzzed through Andre's entire body. Suddenly, his lip was no longer swollen, and his nose stopped bleeding. Andre jumped and backed away with wide eyes. "What's going on? How—how do you know my name?"

The old woman waved her hand in the air. "Oh, that isn't important. What is important is *this* . . ."

With that, the woman opened her black bag and pulled out a small box. It was loosely tied with a dark velvet ribbon, and Andre could have sworn he saw small sparks fly from under the lid.

"This is for you," the old woman said. "You'll know what to do with it," she added mysteriously as she placed the box in Andre's hands. Andre noticed that the box was warm. He peered at it curiously and then raised his head to ask the old woman a question.

But she was gone.

A wind whistled down the street. Andre looked in both directions, but the old woman had simply vanished.

"What a night," Andre murmured as he rubbed his eyes. "I must have gotten a bad knock on my head. I'm seein' things!"

But the box in his hands was real enough. Andre hoped it contained money. He tucked the box under his arm and rushed along the empty street to the safety of his home.

Much later that night, in the privacy of his bedroom, Andre finally opened the box. It was still quite warm to the touch. And when he lifted the lid, Andre thought he saw a stream of sparks fly out. He was certain he heard a low whispering sound.

"What in the world . . ." Andre murmured. Then he stared at the opened box.

Inside, lying side by side, were three small dolls.

"Steve . . . Willie . . . Reggie . . ." Andre said breathlessly as he took them out one at a time. Each doll was dressed exactly as the three boys had been dressed that evening. Each had a sneering, mean expression. Then Andre picked up the last thing in the box: a small felt bag. It was full of gold needles and pins.

"Voodoo dolls!" Andre whispered. Andre had read about voodoo dolls before, but they weren't real . . . or were they? Andre stared at the dolls for a long time. The old woman's words came back to him: *You'll know what to do with it.*

Yes, I will, Andre thought. *I just hope it works.*

The next evening, Andre sat on the front steps of his apartment building for a long time getting his nerve up. The three dolls were stuffed in his pockets, and the needle bag was clenched in his hand. Finally, he took a deep breath and headed toward the alley. Just before turning down the alley, Andre hid behind a doorway and listened. He could hear the three boys laughing meanly.

Slowly, Andre pulled out a gold needle. Then he slipped the Reggie doll out of his pocket. Holding his breath, Andre suddenly plunged the needle into the doll's foot.

"*Aggghhhh!*" Reggie screamed and then cursed loudly. "My foot! Something just stabbed my foot!"

Andre could hardly believe it. It worked! The magic was real! Without losing another second, Andre stuck a needle into Willie's hand and another one into Steve's arm. Soon the alley was echoing with screeches and curses. Then Andre rounded the corner and stood in the alley watching the boys. Reggie looked at

Andre and screamed, "What are you lookin' at, jerk?" while he hopped around on one foot with tears in his eyes.

In response, Andre simply held up the Reggie doll with the pin in its foot. Reggie leaned against the brick wall and stared.

"No way!" Reggie sputtered. "Voodoo ain't real."

"Let's get him," Willie shouted as he shook his stinging hand. "Gonna smash him and his stupid baby dolls, and then . . ."

But before Willie could say anything else, Andre held up the Willie doll and stabbed a needle in its foot. Immediately, Willie fell to the ground, howling and grabbing his foot. Steve began backing away down the alley, a look of terror on his face.

"I'd like my money back," Andre said calmly. "Right now."

"You're crazy," Reggie hissed as he hopped toward Andre with clenched fists. "You ain't gettin' one cent!"

With that, Andre held up the Reggie doll and tapped a needle into its other foot. Reggie fell to the ground, cursing and crying.

Andre walked over and held his hand out. "My money, please."

When Reggie ignored him, Andre pulled

out another needle and positioned it right at the doll's heart.

"No! No!" Reggie screamed. "Here! Take it! Just don't hurt me again!"

Reggie threw a wad of money at Andre's feet. Andre picked it up and looked at the three cowering boys. "If you know what's good for you, you won't ever mess with me or anyone else again," Andre warned. "If you do . . . ," he said as he held up the dolls, "the next needles are going deep into your brains."

"No problem, man," Willie said in a shaking voice. "Whatever you want. Whatever you say."

Then Willie, Reggie, and Steve hobbled and dragged themselves down the alley as fast as they could go in their sorry states. Twice, Reggie looked over his shoulder in terror.

Once they were gone, Andre exhaled a huge sigh of relief. Then he smiled. He walked to the edge of the alley and looked up, hoping the old woman had been out on her balcony watching. But what Andre saw made him gasp. He rubbed his eyes and looked again.

There was no balcony. No window. No cat or candlelight. Instead, there was just the solid brick wall of an old warehouse.

"But how can that be?" Andre whispered to himself.

As if in response, a warm breeze blew down the street. And in the breeze, Andre was certain he smelled a hint of chocolate and cinnamon.

■ ■ ■

Frightened to Death

Out near Black Tree Swamp, there's an opening along a narrow dirt road. If you blink, you might miss it. It almost looks as if someone has carved a tunnel through the thick woods. The opening leads to an old path. Even in the middle of the day, it's pretty gloomy walking along this overgrown path. Spiders run over your feet, and grey Spanish moss hangs from the trees like an old witch's hair. Sometimes there's the distant howling of swamp creatures. Sometimes that howling gets closer and closer.

The dark path eventually leads to a graveyard. But this is not just any graveyard. This graveyard is so old that no one knows when the first person was buried here. Some people believe that it may have been over 300 years ago. Ancient stone markers have crumbled to dust, and even the newer gravestones don't give away too many clues. It's as if the graveyard has secrets it doesn't want anyone to know.

However, there is one tombstone that gives the rare visitor a warning:

> *Keep your distance*
> *From this old stone*
> *Or you'll find yourself*
> *Down here with my bones*

That's the tombstone of old Jasper Vulcan. He died over 150 years ago while fishing for catfish way back in the heart of the swamp. No one knows exactly what happened, but they found several alligators swimming near Jasper's overturned boat. One of the gators had one of Jasper's boots still hanging out of its mouth.

The tale that's been passed around for years says that old Jasper's tombstone had only his name and date of death on it at first. Then there was a terrible lightning storm about a week after Jasper was buried. Trees in the swamp caught on fire, and the whole sky lit up with flames and lightning. Some say that was Jasper showing his anger over getting eaten by alligators. Others say it was just a storm. But whatever it was, the next morning the warning had suddenly appeared on Jasper's tombstone.

And just like that, stories about people disappearing when they visited the ancient graveyard started popping up! Did these people get too close to Jasper's grave? Did a bony hand suddenly plunge out of the damp dirt and grab the intruder by the ankle? No one can say for certain, because no one ever saw anything. However, one young boy swore that his best friend was pulled underground by the ghost of Jasper Vulcan.

"I turned my back for just five seconds," the boy claimed in a newspaper interview in 1889. "And then I heard Buddy scream. When I turned around, he was sinking into the ground fast. He waved his arms like crazy. Then he was gone."

No trace of Buddy was ever found.

Most people figured Buddy got swallowed up by quicksand. But the legend of Jasper's ghost lives on even today. And it still scares some people to death. Consider what happened just last month . . .

"I wouldn't go near that old graveyard on Halloween for anything," Candice said with a shudder. She and several friends were sitting in the school cafeteria eating lunch. It was one week until Halloween, so the talk had turned to all things creepy. Then it turned to taking dares.

"For *anything*?" Brian asked. "Not even for fifty bucks?"

Candice shook her head. "No way. Not even for a hundred."

"I'm with Candice," Joe agreed. "I wouldn't mess around with some place that's haunted. Particularly not on Halloween night. Not with old Jasper's ghost hanging around waiting to grab me."

Emma looked at her friends and rolled her eyes. "You all are ridiculous. There's nothing to be afraid of. It's just some moldy old graveyard. That's all."

"Oh, come on!" Candice said. "You wouldn't go alone into that graveyard on Halloween night, and you know it."

"You're not afraid of ghosts?" Joe asked with a grin. "Wooooooooo!" he added in a high-pitched voice, trying to sound spooky.

"Nope," Emma said as she munched on a carrot. "Ghosts aren't real. The only thing that's real is fear. And I don't have any."

Brian looked around the table. "So, you're saying you'll take the dare, Emma? You'll go alone to the graveyard?"

Tossing her hair back, Emma said, "For fifty dollars, I'll even stand on Jasper Vulcan's grave. No problem."

The other three all stared at each other and then back at Emma.

"Seriously?" Candice almost whispered. "I'd be terrified."

"Not me," Emma said. "This will be the easiest fifty bucks I've ever earned."

One week later, the four friends met up at a Halloween party. Emma was dressed as a witch, with a tall hat and a long black cape that dragged behind her. She thought it would be funny to enter a graveyard as a witch.

"I'll feel right at home," she joked.

"You really are crazy," Joe said, and he shook his head. "But you're way braver than I am."

"And pretty soon, I'll be richer too," Emma added, with a playful punch to Joe's arm.

When the party ended, the four friends rode together in Brian's car toward Black Tree Swamp, chattering excitedly the whole way. But when they turned down the narrow dirt road, everyone grew quiet. Thin white clouds streaked across the moon, and off in the distance a dog howled. Soon, the dark opening to the path appeared. If it had not been for the ghostly moonlight, they would have missed it.

"Are you sure you want to do this?" Brian and Candice asked at the same time. A cool fall wind whistled through the old oak trees, making them creak and sway.

"Yes, I'm sure," Emma said firmly. "I have a flashlight and my magic witch's wand. I couldn't be any safer." Emma giggled, but no one else did.

With that, Emma got out of the car. "I'll be back in about ten minutes," she said. "Don't leave without me!"

Giggling again, Emma headed toward the dark path, her flashlight shining down on the roots and scurrying bugs. Suddenly, she turned back.

"Thank goodness," Candice said with a sigh of relief. She opened the door to let her friend back in the car. But Emma just leaned over and peered in the car window.

"I want to prove that I was standing on Jasper's grave," she said. "I need something to stick in the gravesite. How about your pitchfork, Brian? That way, we can all come back tomorrow in the daylight, and you can see that I did it. Otherwise, it doesn't seem fair to take the money."

"We'll take your word for it," Joe said.

"No way," Emma insisted. "I want to prove it, okay?"

Brian, who was dressed as a devil, complete with a pitchfork, just nodded and handed it over. No one said a word.

Then Emma headed back down the trail. It was an eerie sight to see. A witch in a tall hat and long cape finally faded into the deep swampy darkness.

At first, Emma was truly not afraid at all. *Believing that the ghost of an old fisherman can pull people underground!* she thought. *How lame can you get?* But as she reached the end of the trail and pointed her flashlight into the graveyard, a slight chill went up her spine. Rows of crumbling stones seemed to stare back at her coldly. Emma tried not to think about all the ancient bones buried under her feet as she started to walk into the graveyard.

Moving quickly through the graveyard, Emma searched for Jasper Vulcan's tombstone. Her flashlight bounced across the stones, revealing death date after death date. It began to give her a really creepy feeling.

Just calm down, she told herself. *Ghosts aren't real.*

Suddenly, Jasper's tombstone lit up in the flashlight's beam . . .

Keep your distance
From this old stone
Or you'll find yourself
Down here with my bones

Emma felt her heartbeat quicken, and her mouth went dry. With shaking hands, she walked closer to the edge of Jasper's stone.

Then somewhere just beyond the edge of the darkness, there was a low growling and then a moan. A sudden blast of cold wind blew into Emma's face. It smelled like rot and fear. And then . . . *crunch, crunch, crunch* . . . heavy footsteps were moving toward her! In terror, Emma quickly shoved the pitchfork down on top of Jasper's grave and turned to run.

But something pulled her back.

Emma tugged and yanked and struggled, but whatever was holding her would not let go. Gasping and trying to scream, Emma fell to the ground and clawed at the rocks and roots, trying to pull herself away. The ground seemed to shake and crumble beneath Emma. Her heart was pounding so hard that Emma was suddenly unable to breathe. Something or someone was pulling her down, down, down . . .

When Emma had not returned to the car

after a half hour, her friends were very worried. They had not expected her to take more than five minutes to run out to the graveyard, mark Jasper's grave with the pitchfork, and return.

"We have to go see what's wrong," Candice said in a shaking voice. "Something bad has happened."

For a moment, there was silence in the car. Then Brian grabbed another flashlight that they had brought along "just in case." Without another word, the three friends headed down the dark path. The moon was high overhead and very bright, casting eerie shadows in every direction. When the friends reached the graveyard, the moon was bright enough for them to see the outline of Emma—collapsed and motionless on Jasper's grave.

"Emma!" Brian shouted as they ran over to her. But there was no response.

Kneeling at her side, Brian could see what had happened. Emma had indeed sunk the pitchfork into Jasper's grave, but in her hurry, she had also caught the end of her cape with the pitchfork. That had been what was pulling her back again and again. Now she lay, wide-eyed and lifeless, staring up at the starry October sky.

Emma had frightened herself to death.

■ ■ ■

The Caller

Carla had always enjoyed visiting her Great Aunt Edna. During the summer, for as long as Carla could remember, she always spent two weeks with her aunt. Her aunt could be a little old-fashioned sometimes, but her house was pretty cool. Aunt Edna often told Carla stories about growing up in the house. But as old as Aunt Edna was, her house was much older. And she knew every bit of history about it. Carla loved to hear about the people and families who had lived in the house more than a hundred years ago.

The summer Carla turned 15, Aunt Edna asked Carla if she'd mind staying home alone one evening while Aunt Edna went to dinner with an old friend. Carla was quick to say yes. She felt as though she was certainly old enough to take care of herself. Also, there was a movie on TV that evening that she wanted to watch, and she knew that Aunt Edna wouldn't like it.

"Are you sure you won't be afraid?" Aunt Edna asked.

"Afraid of what?" Carla said with a shrug. "About the most dangerous thing I've ever seen at your house was a deer in the backyard."

"Well, just keep the front door locked," Aunt Edna said in a concerned tone. "You should probably use the old bolt lock, too. That way no one can get in the house."

"Okay," Carla agreed slowly. She hadn't ever thought about someone breaking into her aunt's house.

"And don't go outside after it's dark," her aunt added. "Even on the front porch."

"I won't," Carla said. She wished her aunt had not suggested that danger might lurk outside of the house. Now she did, in fact, feel a little creepy.

That evening, however, Carla watched a beautiful sunset across the fields that ran behind her aunt's house. A late summer thunderstorm was moving in, but it wouldn't be here until much later. After dinner, Carla decided to curl up with a book she wanted to finish reading instead of turning on the TV and ruining the peaceful evening. Just as Carla got comfortable, her cell phone rang. She didn't recognize the number, but she answered anyway.

"Hello?"

On the other end, Carla thought she heard some kind of music playing. It sounded like a violin.

"Hello? Anyone there?" Carla asked.

But then, abruptly, the caller hung up.

Carla sighed and went back to her book. Outside, there were low rumbles of thunder, and then Carla thought she heard a man's voice speaking. She jumped up and peeked out onto the front porch. She didn't see anything, but she turned on a few extra lights anyway. She assured herself that it had only been the thunder.

At that moment, her phone rang again.

"Hello?" Carla said, slightly annoyed.

"Rosemary, this is John. I'll be there soon," a man's voice said. The voice was faint and echoed slightly as if the call was coming in from very far away. However, Carla could see that it was a local call.

"I'm sorry, but you have the wrong

number," Carla explained. "There's no one—"

But the caller had hung up.

"He could have at least apologized," Carla grumbled as she settled back in again with her book.

Outside, the wind was picking up, and it whined around the old house. The walls creaked. A flash of lightning crackled. Carla bit her nails and found it hard to concentrate on what she was reading. Why, oh why did Aunt Edna have to suggest that someone might try to break into the house?

Suddenly Carla's phone rang a second time. Carla jumped and grabbed her phone. It was the same caller *again*!

"Look," Carla began, "you've got the wrong number, so . . ."

"I'm on my way, Rosemary," the man's distant voice interrupted. "It won't be long now." Then the line went dead. Outside, there was a crash of thunder, and rain began tapping on the windows.

Carla felt a chilly wave of fear tingle along her backbone. In a rush, she dashed around and turned *all* the lights on downstairs. Then she went back to the front door and checked the stubborn old bolt lock. It was definitely jammed tight. Nobody would be getting in.

I'm being ridiculous, Carla thought to

herself, and she rolled her eyes as she stood in the middle of the brightly lit living room. However, hearing a strange voice say "I'm on my way" had given her a definite chill. But it was only a wrong number . . .

RING!

Her phone again!

This time, Carla just picked up the call and didn't say anything. She could hear her heart beating in her ears.

"Only minutes away, my dear," the echoing voice whispered. Then the caller laughed like a crazy person, and a violin began playing again.

"Who *is* this?" Carla shouted into her phone. "Stop calling here! You've got the wrong . . ."

Click. The caller hung up again.

Now Carla was angry. Someone was intentionally messing with her. It was probably just some stupid kids making prank calls, and they thought they were scaring her. Well, she'd show them. She'd call them back and tell them they had been calling a police station all along.

"We'll see who's laughing then," Carla muttered as she pulled up the last call on her phone and returned the call.

Then something very weird happened.

At the very moment Carla heard the phone ringing in her cell phone, she also heard an old-fashioned ringing from a phone upstairs. Then someone picked up. And at that same moment, the upstairs ringing stopped.

"Rosemary, I'll be there soon," a distant watery voice whispered.

Carla felt her heart leap. Immediately, she hung up.

What? Carla thought in a panic. *It can't be!*

She called the number again, and again a phone rang upstairs. And it stopped the very second someone picked up.

"I'm coming downstairs now, my dear," the voice wheezed.

"NO!" Carla shrieked as the truth hit her with full force. The calls were coming *from inside the house*! The caller was upstairs!

Now Carla heard slow heavy footsteps overhead. And the footsteps were headed for the stairs. And an eerie violin tune drifted through the house. Outside, a mighty flash of lightning made a crackling sound. Then with a pop, all the lights went out. Carla gasped in fear in the pitch blackness.

Clump . . . clump . . . clump . . .

Carla rushed blindly to the front door. With shaking hands, she fumbled for the rusted old deadbolt lock. It was so dark that she couldn't find it! And the footsteps were getting nearer . . .

Finally, her hand gripped the lock. Carla yanked hard, but it wouldn't budge. It was absolutely jammed into place. With a sickening sense of shock, Carla realized she was locked inside with whoever had been calling.

Clump . . . clump . . . clump . . .

Now the caller began descending the stairs. Each slow, heavy footstep creaked and echoed.

Carla pulled the deadlock and banged it with the palm of her hand until her hand was bleeding. But it remained frozen in place. The footsteps had nearly reached the bottom of the stairs.

"I'm only seconds from you," a high-pitched, echoing voice announced from the landing of the stairs. Then, a crazy laugh rattled through the house.

In desperation, Carla groped her way around the living room until she grasped a heavy iron lamp base. She grabbed it and began pounding it against the deadbolt. She heard footsteps approaching her, but she was too terrified to turn around and look into the darkness behind her. A coldness suddenly filled the room, and the caller's watery and hissing voice now seemed to be right next to her ear.

"Here I am, Rosemary . . . ."

Crash!

The deadbolt finally flew open just as

Carla felt sharp bony fingers digging into her shoulder. Carla threw the front door open and ran out into the front yard screaming.

"Help! Help! No!!"

Someone was grabbing her and holding her tightly. Carla struggled and shrieked and . . .

"Good heavens, Carla! What on earth is wrong?"

It was Aunt Edna. She had just gotten home the moment Carla ran out of the house.

"A man!" gasped Carla as she pointed to the front door. "He . . . he's right there. He was upstairs . . . I . . . I . . ."

But there was no one there. The only sound was the steadily falling rain. No more whispery voice or heavy footsteps. And just like that, the lights came back on.

"But there was someone upstairs," Carla said in confusion. "He kept calling me. Look!"

Carla pulled out her cell phone to show her aunt all the calls that had come from within the house. But every single one of the calls had disappeared. It was as if they had never happened.

"But it *did* happen," Carla insisted. "He said his name was John, and he kept calling me Rosemary, and there was a violin playing . . ."

Aunt Edna looked at her niece for a long moment. All the color slowly drained from her face.

"John and Rosemary Barrow," Aunt Edna finally said with a visible shudder. "They lived in this house nearly a hundred years ago."

"Wha-at?" Carla whispered.

"The story my mother told me was that John won Rosemary's heart with his violin playing," Aunt Edna continued. "But John died suddenly of a heart attack in the back room upstairs. After that, Rosemary moved away."

Carla just stared at her aunt.

"Is that . . ." Carla began shakily. "Do you think that was a ghost? Do you think John's still looking for Rosemary?"

"Well," Aunt Edna said, shaking her head, "I've never believed in ghosts, so I think maybe you just had a bad dream. Perhaps you remember me talking about John and Rosemary. Plus, I had that upstairs phone number disconnected two years ago, so no one could have been calling you from . . ."

RING!

Now Aunt Edna's cell phone was ringing. She dug it out of her purse and looked to see who was calling. She shook her head and murmured, "But that's impossible." Then she looked up at her niece with wide eyes.

"It's coming from upstairs," she whispered.

■ ■ ■

Payback

Ten-year-old Kyle was just about the worst kid in the neighborhood. He stomped through flowers and threw stones at cars. He chased after cats, barking like a crazy dog, and he said rude things to kids smaller than himself. Sometimes he pulled girls' hair until they cried. One time, he even poured an entire can of red paint all the way down the street, because he thought it looked like blood. He hoped it would scare all of his neighbors.

But Kyle's worst favorite thing to do was torture and kill insects. In the middle of the summer, Kyle would take leftover firecrackers from the 4th of July and shove them into anthills. As the ants scurried around, trying to figure out what had just barged into their home, Kyle would carefully strike a match that he had sneaked out of the kitchen. Slowly, he'd light the firecracker. Then he would dash away, giggling with wicked glee.

BANG!

Ants and sand and grass would rocket up into the air. So long, anthill.

"Kyle! Get in here right *now*!"

Kyle's mother would remind him once again how cruel it was to hurt anything, even tiny bugs.

"Why do you keep doing it?" Mom would ask with an annoyed sigh.

"Because it's fun," Kyle would say with a shrug. "Bugs are stupid, anyway. No one cares about stupid bugs."

"Now, that's not true. Why, ants are very important for the soil, because they . . ." Mom would begin. But all Kyle heard was, "Blah blah! blah blah blah!" His mind was already plotting his next insect attack. Perhaps catching a beetle and tying a string around its feet would be amusing. How about pouring salt on slugs? Trapping flies on paper covered with glue?

Finally, one particularly dull afternoon, Kyle came up with the most horrid bug plan yet. Creeping down into the damp, moldy basement of his home, Kyle shone a flashlight in all the darkest and filthiest corners. Ancient cobwebs hung down and stuck to his face, along with bits of long-dead flies. But Kyle wasn't afraid.

"I'm not afraid of anything," Kyle bragged to the empty basement. His voice echoed eerily, and something unseen scuttled away quickly into a corner. "That's right!" Kyle nearly shouted. "I'm so unafraid that I'm the most not-afraid person in the universe."

"In fact," Kyle said slowly as he pointed his flashlight beam into the dirtiest, darkest, most wretched corner of the basement, "I'm not even afraid of . . . YOU!"

Hanging in the very center of an enormous web was the biggest spider Kyle had ever seen. It was black with extra-long jointed legs that twitched and pawed at the strands of the web. Even in the dim light, Kyle could see little bristles of hair on the legs. And were those eyes? Kyle rubbed his own eyes and looked again. In the center of the spider's massive body, Kyle could have sworn he saw two little red glowing eyeballs. And they were staring angrily at Kyle.

"As if," Kyle grumbled, angry that he felt just a tiny, tiny bit afraid. "Spiders don't have glowing eyes." He stepped a bit closer and peered at the spider and quietly added, "Do they?"

The spider suddenly jumped, making the heavy web swing out toward Kyle. The edge of the sticky web clung to Kyle's cheek, and the spider extended one of its eight hairy legs and ran the sharp pointed tip across Kyle's nose.

"Eeeeek!" Kyle screeched as he stumbled backward. Immediately, he clamped his hand over his mouth. Had he just screamed? He looked around nervously, hoping nothing other than the basement had heard him.

"That does it," Kyle barked. He was truly angry at the spider now. He hadn't screamed since his brother had secretly dumped ten live crickets into a box of Cheerios at breakfast time *five years* ago. Nothing scared Kyle anymore— particularly not some stupid spider. That spider was going to pay.

Kyle pulled out a sturdy paper bag from under his arm and opened it up. When he pushed it into the web, the web tore apart, sounding like soggy paper ripping. Hollow bugs that had been the spider's past dinners fluttered to the floor. It kind of grossed Kyle out. However, Kyle was pleased to see the spider back up to a corner of its web for a moment and then scurry directly into the darkness of the bag.

"What an idiot," Kyle said proudly. He quickly folded the top of the bag down to trap the spider. Hearing the spider scuttling around in confusion inside the bag made Kyle smile. He promptly bounded across the basement to a hidden corner. In the corner were a wobbly table and an old lamp. Kyle liked to think of this corner as his private laboratory. He often performed "interesting" operations on everything from bugs to dead mice here. He had even managed to steal a sharp-edged screwdriver to help with his operations. With a sparkle in his eye, Kyle slowly opened the paper bag . . .

It is enough to say that when Kyle was finished with this particular operation, the doomed spider was in nine different pieces. Eight legs were lined up neatly on a salad plate that Kyle had stolen from the kitchen last week. And the large body rolled around on the plate like a black mushy grape.

"Not staring at me anymore, are you, you jerk?" Kyle crowed. He folded his arms and stared at the spider parts with satisfaction. After a while, Kyle yawned. He was already bored with his most recent adventure.

"Is it dinnertime yet?" Kyle bellowed as he went stomping back upstairs. Although pulling spiders apart would ruin most people's appetites for at least a week, Kyle ate three servings of spaghetti that evening. After having a lengthy burping contest with his brother and watching an old *Spiderman* movie, Kyle finally went to bed. It had been a great day.

BOOM!

A tremendous crack of thunder woke Kyle up with a start. His mouth felt dry, and his heart was hammering. What had he been dreaming? He couldn't remember exactly, but it seemed as if there had been something sticky and stinky in it. And there had definitely been some sharp bloody fangs in it. *Stupid*, Kyle thought as his heart slowed its beating.

As the storm moved on and the night grew deathly quiet, Kyle began drifting back to sleep. But now a new and odd sound began creeping into Kyle's brain.

Scratch, click, scratch, click, click . . .

Kyle opened one eye.

Scraaaaaaatch . . .

What *was* that? Kyle sat up in his bed and tried to figure out where the sound was coming from. Everything was silent for a few minutes. Then there was a sudden loud scraping noise that made Kyle jump. It sounded as if it was coming from the large air vent across his room. Kyle grabbed his flashlight and directed the beam toward the vent. Instantly, there was a loud skittering sound that seemed to fade and then disappear far down in the vent.

Kyle leaned down and peered into the air vent. A cold puff of air came out. And along with it was a damp, scary smell. It smelled like mold mixed with rotting food. The hair stood up on the back of Kyle's neck as he slowly backed away from the vent. Then a sudden thought occurred to him.

Of course it's stinky, he said to himself with a sigh of relief. *The vents go straight down to the basement. Everything's gross down there.*

The noise had probably just been the wind or something. Maybe a leaf had gotten blown into the vent. Everything always seemed noisier at night. Reassured, Kyle immediately fell back to sleep with a loud snore. But sometime, much later, in the deepest part of the night, something kept coming to Kyle in his dream. A hand or a tree branch or a sharp piece of wire . . . *something* was tickling and then scratching his cheek. Half asleep, Kyle reached up to brush it away and . . .

"*ARRRGGGH!* Get *off!*"

Kyle slapped frantically at his cheek. At that very moment, whatever had been touching him scurried away. There was more skittering noise in the vent, and then there was dead silence, except for Kyle's pounding heart. What was going on? Kyle rubbed a place on his cheek where he was sure something had been crawling on him. He could still feel the prickling scratchiness, and he shuddered to think of how big it (whatever *it* was!) had felt. Even though it was the middle of July, Kyle's room had suddenly gone cold. He pulled a blanket over his head and tried to calm down. Bit by bit, Kyle convinced himself that it had just been a dream.

"Dreams are lame," he muttered as he relaxed. "And being scared of dreams is the lamest." Kyle decided that it must have been something he ate before he went to bed. No more super-hot fireballs after dinner.

The next day, Kyle found himself bored as usual. Then he remembered his pulled-apart spider downstairs. Excited to see what dried-up spider parts looked like, Kyle zipped back down to his laboratory. But to his disappointment, the spider was gone. In fact, the screwdriver was gone too.

"Oh great," Kyle sighed. "Mom's discovered my top-secret lab. I'm in big trouble now. *Huge* trouble!"

At that moment, Kyle felt a chilly breeze creep up eerily around him. He jumped a little and spun around. Nothing. But what was the basement window doing wide open? Kyle couldn't remember opening it yesterday, but maybe he had. Or maybe it had blown open during the storm. That would explain the weird noises last night. Squirrels and raccoons had gotten into the basement before when a window was left open, and one time a mouse had even gotten into the air vents.

Kyle reached up to latch the window shut and . . .

"UGH!"

Along the ledge and stuck in the edges were some large hairy bristles. Worse than that, there was greenish slime dripping down one side. The slime smelled like week-old garbage.

"Must have been a skunk," Kyle grumbled as he shut the window and quickly wiped the slime off of his arm with an old rag.

For the rest of the day, Kyle kept expecting his mother to yell at him, but she never did. In fact, she made his favorite dinner and even let him stay outside later than usual that evening. Had his mother simply forgotten? Did she not even care about his bug lab? Happily, Kyle used the extra time outside to throw a rock at a robin and trap seventeen fireflies in a jar. Then he dropped a huge June bug down the back of his brother's shirt, ate an extra-large bag of gummy worms, and watched a scary television show about zombies. Kyle finally flopped down in bed exhausted. It had been the perfect day.

But it would be far from the perfect night.

Kyle was sleeping so soundly that he never heard the skittering and scuttling coming up the air vent from the basement. And Kyle snored right through the screws on the air vent in his room being unscrewed one by one. The cold air and rotten smell that filled his room did not wake him up. Only when the vent cover clanged to the floor did Kyle roll over, still half asleep.

Click, click, scraaaatch . . .

"What? Huh?" Kyle mumbled as he opened his eyes. Then, in a flash, his heart felt like it had frozen.

Staring back at Kyle from the vent opening were two huge red eyes. They didn't blink. They just stared at Kyle. And the pulsing red glow from the eyes made just enough light to reveal what was making the clicking noise. Beneath the eyes, a broad wet mouth was set in a large round body, and in the mouth, sharp fangs and teeth glimmered.

Click, click . . . the fangs snapped together quickly.

Then with a prickly scratching noise, a long hairy leg reached forward out of the vent. Then another . . . and another . . . and . . .

Spider! Kyle thought in terror. But he had never seen a spider this big. It was ghastly, an exact mega-sized version of the spider he had killed. The legs were as long as his own legs. In the red light, he could see the hairy bristles and the sharp claw at the end of each leg. Now all eight legs had pushed through the vent, and the massive monster spider stood up. It was taller than Kyle! Slowly, the spider moved in jerky sideways movements toward Kyle. It extended one of its long legs inches from Kyle's face.

Kyle tried to scream, but no sound came out. He tried to move, but he was frozen with panic.

The spider crawled onto Kyle's bed and hovered over him.

Click . . . click . . .

Suddenly, a disgusting green slime poured from the spider's mouth and began covering Kyle. Then threads as strong as steel began to surround him, wrapping him tighter and tighter. The spider's legs all worked together to form a sticky, horrible cocoon around Kyle from head to foot. Only a small opening was left around his eyes so that he could see all the terrors that were to come.

"NO! NOOOO!" Kyle finally managed to sputter. But it was too late. The spider quickly picked Kyle up in its fangs and scuttled back to the vent. Kyle was wrapped so tightly that he slid all the way down to the basement. The monster spider scurried down behind him, promptly grasped Kyle in his fangs again, and crawled up the wall and out the reopened window into the midnight moonlight. It sprang across the damp grass on its giant legs. It drooled hungrily.

Up, up, up . . . The spider ran sideways up a huge oak tree. Kyle tried to move, to speak, to do anything. But he couldn't. Some of the green slime had slid into his eyes and mouth. And now it seemed to be making him numb and very sleepy.

This is just a dream, Kyle kept repeating in his mind. *Just a stupid dream. That's why I'm sleepy. I'll wake up in a little bit. That's the way dreams always are.*

But *was* it a dream?

Kyle realized he was being carried to the center of a massive spider web. The sticky web was as big as his bedroom, and it waved eerily in the silver moonlight. And surrounding the web, on the branches of the trees, were huge fireflies, slugs, flies, ants, and one very angry-looking June bug.

Now the clicking fangs of the spider inched toward Kyle's neck. And the bugs on the branches seemed to move in closer, all of them buzzing and clicking and snapping until it reached a roar.

"Help! Help!" Kyle barely managed to whisper as he drifted helplessly toward sleep.

The last thing Kyle saw was some kind of design or letters written into the weaving of the gigantic spider web. Kyle squinted through the slime at it. He could barely make it out. Finally he was able to bring it into a hazy focus. It was one word:

Payback.

Kyle gasped. Then everything went dark.

■ ■ ■

The Deal with Dr. Lucifer

Danny Michaels fought back angry tears as he hurried away from his homeroom class in humiliation. Laughter from the classroom echoed down the hallway and followed him as he looked for a place to hide. Danny had never exactly been Mr. Popular at his school, but he had never been a total loser either. Most days rolled along without any problems or embarrassments or hassles. Some days even passed by without anyone bothering him at all aside from teachers asking complicated questions or old Roberta, the cafeteria lady, asking him whether he wanted salad or fries. Sometimes Roberta even sneaked Danny second helpings. But most of the kids didn't even take a second look at Danny, the tall skinny sophomore with red hair. And Danny was usually okay with that.

But when his mom brought home a pair of Lunar G-Force shoes from the monthly church clothes giveaway, Danny was suddenly the center of attention in his morning homeroom class. The first twenty minutes of school on Monday morning had been great as, one by one, classmates gathered around to stare at the flashy, expensive basketball shoes. Then, with a wave of dread, Danny noticed Jake Smith staring at him from the other side of homeroom with a mean grin.

"Are those *my* shoes?" Jake shouted with a sharp laugh.

Danny's proud conversation with his classmates stopped dead. He gulped silently and took a deep breath. Then he suddenly broke out into a cold sweat. The letters "J.S." had been written inside of each shoe. He hadn't thought anything about it, since these were used shoes, but now he realized whose initials those were. The chances that he would get Jake's used shoes were about one in a million.

Why, why, why? Danny moaned in his head. Jake was a big star on the JV basketball team, but he could be a serious jerk toward anyone who was different or shy or afraid of him. Making matters even worse, Jake's family was rich, and Jake got a new pair of unbelievable over-the-top basketball shoes about every six months. So there was no doubt about whose shoes these were. And, now, making matters the very worst they could be, Jake was walking over to Danny's desk with a smirk on his face.

"Hey, I asked you a question, string bean," Jake barked. "Are those my old Lunars?"

"No . . . uh . . . no," Danny stammered. "I've . . . had these . . . for like . . . a long time." Danny hated that he was afraid of Jake. He was actually a few inches taller than Jake, but Danny always felt like a stupid little kid when Jake decided to pick on him. Even though Danny didn't like Jake, sometimes he wished he could be more like him. It would be nice to be popular and confident for a change.

"Oh, *sure* you have," Jake sneered. "If by 'a long time' you mean since your mommy picked them up for you at the church clothing giveaway yesterday."

Suddenly, Jake lunged toward the floor,

grabbing Danny's foot, pulling it up, and trying to yank the shoe off. The homeroom teacher, Mr. Chambers, was still down the hall making copies, so Jake threw Danny to the floor and wrestled him until he finally ripped a shoe off Danny's foot. Then Jake pranced around the classroom, holding the shoe in the air like a trophy and laughing. Pretty soon, all the kids in the class were staring at Danny.

"THEY *ARE* MY SHOES!!!" Jake bellowed after a quick glance inside the shoe. "My initials are right here!"

That's when Danny jumped up, grabbed the sneaker back from Jake and ran out of the classroom with one shoe in his hand and one on his foot. Everyone in his homeroom was pointing at him and laughing.

"Check it out!" Jake shouted above the laughter. "Danny's wearing my stinky old used-up shoes! How gross can you get?"

Quickly running down the hallway, Danny tried to think of where he could hide for at least the next few hours. Turning a corner, he stopped short. Standing at her locker with her back turned was Brooke Willow. She was one of the prettiest girls in the whole school, and one of the only ones that were ever nice to Danny. She sometimes spoke to Danny and even smiled at him for no reason at all.

Although he would never tell a soul, Danny had had a crush on Brooke since the fifth grade. But all the guys had a crush on her—particularly Jake. And Danny knew he couldn't compete with someone as popular as Jake, so he never even tried.

Danny darted across the hall to the boys' bathroom before Brooke could see him. Breathing a sigh of relief, he splashed a little water on his face, took a deep breath, and put on the other shoe. Maybe by lunch, everyone would have forgotten. With any luck, only old Roberta with her toothless smile would speak to him again today.

Danny paced the floor of the bathroom, angrily talking to himself.

"Anyone," Danny muttered bitterly. "I wish I could be *anyone* other than me. I hate my life and the way I am!"

Suddenly, something struck Danny lightly on the forehead. Looking down, he saw a small diamond-shaped piece of red paper flutter to tile floor. Danny stopped walking and glanced sharply at the ceiling. No one else was in the bathroom. Carefully, Danny picked up the piece of paper. It was still warm, as though it had just left someone's hands.

"*Doctor Lucifer*," Danny read quietly. "*Dealer of Dreams.*"

"And I do believe Danny has a dream," a deep voice boomed, startling Danny.

Danny jumped back and banged his head against one of the bathroom stalls. Then he held his breath and listened, his eyes darting around the room. The bathroom was dead still. Was he losing his mind?

Then, very slowly, a black cloud started to swirl and fill one of the mirrors across from Danny. The surface of the glass started to turn to a jelly-like substance and began dripping down the tile walls. Danny's mouth fell open, and he leaned slowly forward, gawking at the melting mirror. Then, suddenly, the cloud in the mirror started to take shape, coming together in an eerie human form. Two glowing orange eyes appeared, and beneath the eyes, a large mouth widened.

"Good morning, young man!" the voice boomed from inside the melting glass. Danny jumped backward again and almost lost his balance.

"Who—what is that?" Danny gasped as he backed away. In a flash, a huge leathery arm reached out through the rippling glass, five sharp claws tipping the gleaming snakelike skin. Danny shrieked and fell back against the stall door.

All at once, the monster arm transformed

into a harmless human arm clothed in a well-tailored suit. "Doctor Lucifer at your service, of course," the voice said more quietly. But now the voice had a weird haunting sound that made Danny uneasy. For a long moment, Danny didn't speak as he stood shaking against the bathroom stall.

"It's all right, Danny," the voice echoed. "I know I can help you. I think you'll like what I have to offer."

A very tall man in a dark suit slowly stepped out of the melting mirror and into the bathroom. He had a short pointed beard and strange red eyes. He grinned broadly at Danny, but Danny wasn't sure the grin looked very friendly.

"I see that you've been having a few problems, Danny," Dr. Lucifer said calmly, staring down at Danny. "I hear that you'd like your life to be different."

Danny just shrugged and looked nervously around the bathroom. Was this some kind of joke?

"Well, my friend, I think I might be able to strike up a deal with you," Dr. Lucifer smiled. The smile was so dazzling that Danny could not look away. In a quick movement, Dr. Lucifer snapped his fingers over his head. There was a flash of light and a soft popping sound, and a small box instantly appeared in the doctor's hand. The box was covered in red satin, and Danny noticed that the bathroom suddenly smelled like candy and cookies and hot chocolate.

"What is that?" Danny barely whispered as he pointed at the box.

"This," Dr. Lucifer began as he stepped close to Danny and flipped open the top of the box, "is the answer to all your problems, Danny."

Inside the box were five candies wrapped in black cellophane. The delicious scent rising from the box was better than anything Danny had ever smelled. Helpless to control himself, Danny reached for one of the candies, but Dr. Lucifer tapped Danny's hand away. Danny jumped. Dr. Lucifer's touch had felt like a quick sting or the touch of a hot match head.

"Listen carefully, my friend," the doctor said in a low rumble. "Each time you eat a candy, you will get one step closer to that 'someone else' you long to be. All your desires will become realities."

Danny nodded. He couldn't wait to eat one of those candies!

"But you must eat *every single candy*. And pay close attention to the wrapper," Doctor

Lucifer murmured. "One minute after eating the candy, a simple command will appear. You must—I repeat, you *must*—follow the command. If you don't finish the candies and follow each command . . ."

The doctor suddenly stared deep into Danny's eyes. Danny felt his stomach turn and the skin on the back of his neck tingle.

"If you don't, you will instantly return to this very moment in time, hiding in this bathroom, crying and wishing you were someone else," Dr. Lucifer growled. "Don't make that terrible mistake, Danny. Do we have a deal?"

Danny nodded again and whispered, "Yes."

Then as Danny reached up for the small box, the doctor's eyes began blazing like two hot coals. He locked eyes with Danny, and Danny felt a cold, slimy horror roll through him.

"I do not take kindly to deal breakers," Dr. Lucifer said, his voice dropping to a ghastly hollow boom. "If I were you, Danny, I'd remember that."

Then the strange doctor grinned his horrible grin so widely that Danny could see rows of knife-sharp teeth gleaming. Slowly, Dr. Lucifer faded away, leaving only two glowing eyeballs. Finally, the eyeballs turned into a watery mist that blew damply over Danny and then, with a *whoosh*, flew out the open window above the sink.

Danny stared at the box that was now in his trembling hands. A bell rang, and Danny heard kids pile into the hall. Just outside the bathroom door, someone shouted, "Hey, did you hear about Danny's shoes? It's hilarious!"

Without another moment's hesitation, Danny unwrapped a candy and popped it in his mouth. It was unlike anything he had ever tasted. Something like fire, wind, confidence, and strength, all swirled with sugar and fudge, trickled down Danny's throat. It was incredibly delicious and exhilarating. A cool breeze seemed to flow through him, and suddenly Danny couldn't wait to face the kids in the hall. The joke about his shoes seemed like a world away.

Almost as an afterthought, Danny glanced down at the black wrapper. Slowly, a message was appearing in red, as if someone was writing as he watched.

Make a joke about someone who looks funny.

Danny read it again. That seemed like a strange command. *But it won't be a problem*, Danny thought confidently as he strode out of the bathroom. Suddenly, out of the corner of his eye, Danny saw something weird. A grainy shadow seemed to be following him, but there wasn't enough light in the hall to create a shadow. Danny whipped his head around, and the shadow was suddenly gone. A low rumbling laugh faded near his ears.

"Whatever," Danny murmured with a shrug. The magical candy had instantly made him feel brave, strong, and confident. Who cared about a stupid shadow? As Danny moved down the hall, he held his head high; and if other students snickered at him, he looked them right in the eye until they looked away in confusion. No one had ever seen Danny Michaels swagger with that kind of attitude.

As everyone settled into their seats in history class, Jake smirked and called, "Hey Danny, how do MY shoes feel?"

Before anyone could even laugh, Danny shot back, "Kinda tight, Jake. You might want to grow a few inches if you wanna play varsity basketball, shorty."

For a moment the whole class was stunned. No one ever talked back to Jake Smith. Danny looked around at the shocked faces and grinned. A few of the less popular students grinned back at him and gave him nods of approval. Even Brooke smiled. Jake didn't say a word. In fact, his face turned red, and he looked upset. He turned back around and sat with his arms folded, frowning throughout the class.

Wow! This is so awesome! Danny thought to himself. *So this is how it feels to be someone else.* In that same instant, the vague shadow rolled by again, and a low, demonic laugh rumbled just outside Danny's left ear. Danny shuddered for a moment, but nothing was going to ruin this newfound awesomeness.

When lunchtime rolled around, Danny stood in line cracking jokes with a few older boys he'd barely ever spoken to before. When they got to Roberta, Roberta gave Danny her toothless smile. But Danny just turned around to the older boys and said loudly, "I'd pay fifty bucks to watch Roberta try and eat corn on the cob." The boys burst out laughing. Danny felt a chilly tingle roll down his spine, and something that felt like a icy hand clutched his shoulder. A small voice breathed the word *excellent* in his ear. It sounded like applause.

Roberta just closed her mouth quickly and stopped smiling at everyone. She looked at Danny with a confused expression and shook her head. Her reaction made Danny feel a little unsure of himself, so he secretly reached into his backpack for the satin box. Popping another candy into his mouth, Danny felt an even greater surge of power and confidence.

A dull roar seemed to rumble in his head, as if engines were firing up. So what if he had told a little joke about Roberta? The cool kids always did stuff like that. Now Danny looked down at the black wrapper. Glowing red ink slowly appeared.

Take something from someone smaller than you.

Danny chuckled. This would be easy *and* fun. The rumbling in his head was making him feel almost a little dangerous. It was a great feeling. The older boys asked Danny to sit with them during lunch. Danny looked around the cafeteria and noticed that some of the kids were looking at him curiously. *That's right!* Danny thought. *It's the new Danny. Better not mess with me!*

"Yep, this is gonna be a blast," Danny murmured happily to himself as he bit into a cheeseburger. At that moment, he remembered the command, so he glanced around at the kids sitting near him.

"Hey shrimp, where'd you get that cookie?" Danny asked a skinny younger kid sitting one table over. "I didn't see any like that in the lunch line."

The small boy was holding a huge chocolate chip cookie. "My mom made it," the boy said nervously. "It's . . . it's my birthday."

"Well, you'd better leave room for cake, then," Danny said as he popped out of his seat, snatched the cookie out of the boy's hands, and took a huge bite. One of the older boys laughed loudly and slapped Danny on the back.

A hollow, echoing voice hissed right outside of Danny's ear: *Yesssssssss!! Way to go!!!* Danny could even feel hot breath on his neck. He looked over his shoulder, half expecting to see Dr. Lucifer standing next to him and applauding. But all he saw was the smaller boy frowning with tears in his eyes. Instead of making Danny feel bad, it now made him feel strong. He finished off the cookie with a wide smile.

"Dude, that's not cool," one of the older boys suddenly said. "How would you like it if someone did that to your little brother?"

Danny just shrugged and rolled his eyes. But somewhere deep inside, a glimmer of regret lit up in Danny. Had what he'd done been wrong? As Danny walked to class, he unwrapped another candy and ate it quickly. This time, a high-pitched whistle and siren wailed in his head as a terrific rush of heat and strength blew through him. Danny's heart raced so fast, he thought it might explode. Although he was only walking down a crowded hallway, Danny felt like he was flying. It was awesome. When he came up behind Brooke, Danny suddenly put his arm around her.

"Hey, babe! How's it going? You lookin' for me?"

Danny was surprised when Brooke pulled away and gave him a funny look. Wasn't she thrilled to have *Danny Michaels* paying attention to her? Danny just laughed and said, "Catch you later, girl." He knew she would not be able to resist him soon. By the time he finished all the candies, Danny was certain he'd be the most popular kid in his school. Danny glanced at the empty wrapper in his hand.

Cheat on your algebra test.

Danny snorted a laugh out loud and shook his head. That was the easiest one yet. It would be a breeze to cheat in Mr. Snyder's class. Old Snyder never even looked up from his desk during tests, and Danny had often seen other kids cheat. Now Danny couldn't remember why he'd never cheated in the past. It would have been way easier than studying! As Danny positioned himself at a desk behind the smartest girl in his class and copied all her answers, a low rumble like a huge crowd cheering louder and louder filled his ears. A flood of hot electric power surged through him. Danny had never felt so powerful.

By the end of the school day, Danny truly believed there wasn't anything he couldn't do. All the kids in his class seemed to be in awe of him, staring wide-eyed with their mouths hanging open at everything Danny was doing. And Jake was staying as far away from Danny as possible. It was all incredible, except . . .

Out of the corner of his eye again, Danny could sense something like a rolling bank of dark fog rushing in from behind him every time he ate another candy. Worse than that, Danny could feel a pair of eyes on him, intently focusing like the eyes of a hunter on its prey. And worst of all, Danny felt as though his shadow was no longer his own. It was more of an evil darkness that seemed to follow him everywhere.

And once, when he glanced at his reflection in a classroom window, Danny did not recognize the boy staring back. It looked like him or, at least, some sort of horrific version of him. The reflection grinned back with a wide, fang-filled mouth and glowing red eyes. Danny had shuddered and looked away quickly.

Later that night, as he lay awake in bed, Danny felt a tingling of terror bubbling up beneath all his newfound confidence. What was happening to him? What was he becoming? What was in those crazy candies anyway? Danny was beginning to feel as if he was trapped in a nightmare and couldn't wake up.

Maybe I should just stop eating the candies, Danny thought just before sunrise. *After all, there's no way that Lucifer dude can really make me go back in time. I'm already changed enough, I think.*

A blasting *whoosh* of hot air suddenly filled Danny's room. It smelled like sulfur and burning rubber. Then, two huge dark eyeballs appeared and floated in the air just above Danny's head. The eyes looked furious. They changed from black to burning red, and then a harsh voice hissed, "We have a deal, Danny. If you break it, you will return to your sad old unpopular self! And that is only the beginning of the horrors you will face! You *must* finish the candies!!"

Danny's eyes, bloodshot from the sleepless night, shot open wide as he suddenly felt two cold hands pressing down against his shoulders. Danny struggled, but the icy hands pinned him to his bed. The odor in his room now changed to the smell of something dead and rotting. The grainy shadow that seemed to have been following Danny around slowly settled on top of Danny, its hands digging into his shoulders. Danny felt as if a huge bucket of cold slime had just been poured on him.

"I'd like you to meet my friend," Dr. Lucifer's evil voice whispered in Danny's ear. "I'm sure you've noticed him hanging around. Unless you want him to be your constant shadow, I strongly suggest you finish those candies. A deal is a deal. Of course, if you'd rather not keep your end of the bargain, I can have my friend put his hands around your neck and . . ."

"All right!" Danny cried out in desperation. "I'll do it!"

Instantly, the shadow evaporated with a hiss. Freed, Danny immediately jumped out of bed and rushed for his bedroom door. It slammed shut on its own. He spun around now, trapped in his room with Dr. Lucifer's huge blazing eyeballs. A low, rumbling laughter echoed in Danny's ears, and it became louder and louder until Danny felt as though his head would explode.

"Perhaps I didn't make myself clear," Dr. Lucifer snarled. With an angry roar, the cold shadow reappeared and wrapped itself around Danny. Slimy, cold fingers slid around Danny's throat.

"No! Give me the candy!" Danny managed to choke out.

The red satin box floated across the room and into Danny's trembling hands. Grabbing one of the last two candies, Danny popped it in his mouth and swallowed it whole. Instantly, the slime shadow vanished. Clanging bells and screaming wind roared in Danny's head, and a sensation like riding the biggest roller coaster on earth stormed through Danny's body along with huge waves of incredible strength and confidence. Danny instantly forgot his terror and his worries about the candy. He looked at the wrapper.

Demand whatever you want from everyone.

"Ha!" Danny laughed. "This one will be a most fun yet. The most popular guy at school *always* gets what he wants, and that's totally me. This day is going to be the best!"

After completely ignoring his parents and brother at breakfast, Danny hopped on the school bus. Immediately, he forced a young girl with braces out of her seat. He wanted that seat. Walking to homeroom, he shoved two students from behind. They were in his way. Then he saw Brooke standing at her locker with her back to him. He crept up right behind her and said, "Hey there!"

"What?" Brooke said, whirling around.

When she saw Danny, she looked both confused and embarrassed. "You surprised me."

"Yeah, well, here comes an even bigger surprise," Danny said confidently. "Why don't we go to the school dance together next Friday? You'll have a great time with *me*!"

Brooke stared at Danny with a funny expression on her face. Then she frowned and shook her head.

"No way, Danny."

"Wh-what?" Danny asked in disbelief. "Why wouldn't you want to go with me?"

"Because you're suddenly acting so weird and rude. You're like Jake or some of those other boys that I can't stand," Brooke replied. She just shrugged and added, "I miss the old Danny."

With that, Brooke turned back to her locker.

Danny's mind raced in circles. Why wasn't Brooke impressed with him? How in the world could she have liked the *old* pathetic Danny better? What was wrong with her anyway? Why weren't the candies working?

Danny felt that faint glimmer of regret and confusion glowing deep inside. Then he looked over at Brooke as she slowly pulled books out of her locker. The glow inside grew stronger. Brooke's words repeated themselves over and over in Danny's head. *I miss the old Danny . . . the old Danny . . . the old Danny . . .*

"It's not right," Danny finally whispered shakily to himself. "I—I can't eat the final candy."

A sudden sharp thunderclap banged in Danny's ears. The school hallway seemed to fade into black bit by bit, as if someone were dimming the lights.

Standing in the complete darkness with his heart racing, Danny heard something huge slithering on the floor toward him. Danny tried running, but his legs felt frozen in place. Then, in a flash of hot light, Dr. Lucifer appeared in his true form. His dark snakelike skin shimmered, and jagged fangs flashed. The doctor's glowing eyes focused on Danny, and a forked tongue shot out with a hiss.

"We had a deal!" the doctor said as he stepped toward Danny, his clawed hands reaching out for Danny's throat.

Danny shut his eyes and took a deep breath. "I want the old Danny back," he whispered again and again as he slowly reached in his back pocket, clutched the last candy, and unwrapped it.

"The old Danny is a loser!" the doctor hissed. Danny could feel the sharp tips of claws on his neck. "Nobody likes him! Everyone makes fun of—"

"I . . . I want to be me! I *like* me!" Danny suddenly shouted angrily as he reached out to shove Dr. Lucifer away with one hand. Danny's other hand flew out of his pocket. With all his strength, Danny threw the candy into Dr. Lucifer's huge mouth and down his throat. The doctor looked stunned for a moment, and then he shrieked and grabbed at his throat. But it was too late. The candy was gone. The deal was over.

"NO!" Dr. Lucifer howled.

There was a shattering sound like hundreds of breaking bottles, and black smoke billowed around Danny. Then the hallway floor instantly disappeared, and Danny was hurtling through space at rocket speed. The speed was so intense that he felt as if the skin on his face was peeling off. Danny began spinning uncontrollably, and then everything started fading far, far away . . .

Bonk!

Danny reached up to rub his head. It had hit something hard and cool. Rubbing his eyes, Danny realized he was in the boys' bathroom. A bell rang, and Danny heard kids pile into the hall. Just outside the bathroom door, someone shouted, "Hey, did you hear about Danny's shoes? It's hilarious!"

"I'm back!" Danny said out loud in the empty bathroom. "I'm me again!" He couldn't remember the last time he'd felt this relieved and happy. He understood that everything had returned to the way it had been before he ate the candies. He had not intimidated Jake, but neither had he cruelly insulted Roberta, stolen a younger boy's cookie, cheated on a test, or been too familiar with Brooke. Everything was as it was—yet he had learned a lesson he would not forget.

Out in the hall again, Danny noticed Brooke at her locker and walked shyly over to her and waved an awkward hello.

"Hi, Danny," Brooke said with a warm smile. "What's new?"

"Well, I . . . um . . ." Danny began. "I wondered if you . . . um . . . that is, if you'd like to go to the dance . . ."

At that very moment, Jake walked close by, smirked at Danny, and said, "Nice shoes, loser!"

"Sure, I'd love to go to the dance with you, Danny!" Brooke said loudly enough for Jake to hear. "That would be great."

Jake did a double take and frowned. "You gotta be kidding me," he mumbled jealously. "No way."

Brooke just ignored Jake and grabbed Danny's hand. As she did, a crumpled black candy wrapper fell to the floor. With satisfaction, Danny stepped on it as he and Brooke headed to history class.

What a great day to be me, Danny thought happily.

■ ■ ■

Robin and the Vampire

"**Y**ou need to come home right away," Robin's mother cried over the phone. "Your baby brother is so sick that we're not sure he's going to make it."

"*What?*" Robin asked in a stunned voice. "What's happened? Harry never gets sick!"

"The doctors can't figure it out," her mother said miserably. "He was fine until yesterday. He had been outside playing in the back yard just after dark when he said something stung him. He said it was a huge bug that just appeared out of nowhere."

"A huge bug? What kind of bug?"

"That's the problem. The doctors can't tell," Robin's mother said through tears. "Harry has these two red sting marks on his neck. There doesn't seem to be any infection, but Harry keeps getting weaker and weaker. It's as if the life is just draining out of him!"

"I'm on my way," Robin said. "Tell Harry that I'll be home before dark. Tell him that I promise."

Robin was in college on the other side of the state, but if she hurried, she could catch the last train back home. Then from the train station, it was just a few miles to her parents' house. Robin grabbed a few things, shoved them in her backpack, and flew out the door. Harry was her only brother, and though she and Harry were twelve years apart in age, the two of them were unusually close. Robin would do anything for her little brother.

When Robin finally reached the train stop near her parents' house, she tried calling her parents three times, but no one answered. Was Harry worse? Were they at the hospital? Robin's mind spun with stressful questions as she bit her nails. She looked out in front of the station for a cab, but the streets were empty.

Even the station was empty except for a young man reading a book at the ticket counter. Robin rushed to the counter.

"Excuse me, sir," Robin said. "Do you know if I can get a cab or some kind of ride over to Grassland Street? It's kind of an emergency."

The young man stared at Robin. He had long dark hair and piercing gold eyes. He stared at Robin for so long that she felt a little embarrassed but also a little flattered. Finally, he stood up and said, "No cabs for another 45 minutes. There's really not enough business here to keep any out front, so one just shows up on the hour."

Robin sighed and looked out the window. It was already nearly twilight. She had promised Harry she'd be home before dark. Without a second thought, Robin opened her backpack and pulled out a pair of running shoes. She competed in track at college and was one of the fastest milers on the team. She figured she should be able to run the three miles home before it was dark.

Suddenly, the young man approached her. "What are you doing?" he asked with a worried frown.

"I'm going to run home," Robin replied as she finished tying the laces. "I can't wait

45 minutes. I can run home way faster than that."

The man looked around the station, and then he leaned over and spoke in a low voice as though he was telling Robin a secret.

"I wouldn't do that if I were you, if you don't mind my saying so."

Robin just shook her head without looking up. "I have to. My little brother's really sick. He may not make it through the night."

"A bite on the neck?"

Robin looked up sharply. "What? How could you know that?"

"That's what I'm trying to tell you," the man said. "You need to know that there's a . . ."

He paused and glanced around the station again. Robin thought it looked as though he was listening closely to make sure no one was nearby. He even cocked his head. "What I mean to say," the strange young man continued in a hushed voice, "is that some people are claiming that young people and children are being hunted."

Robin stared at the young man in shocked disbelief. "Hunted? What do you mean?"

"You know the tall mountain just south of this station?" the man asked as he pointed in the direction of the hills. "There's an old woman living somewhere up there. It's thought that the woman is a . . . a vampire."

"No way," Robin murmured. "A vampire living on Diablo Mountain? Someone's just making things up."

"I wouldn't be so sure," the man said quietly. "There have been deaths, unexplained deaths. They say that this woman rises from her resting place on the mountain just after dark and seeks out young people. She takes their young blood so that she can make her old life last longer. It's believed that she hunts in the form of a bat. Then all she needs is a bite on the neck, a long drink of blood, and . . ."

Robin was staring at the man in horror. "And then what?" she asked.

"Then she returns to her vampire form, full of incredible strength. And unless this vampire woman is killed, her victim will die within in three days."

Robin gasped. Could it be true? Harry had been bitten on the neck just after dark by something he thought was a huge bug!

Now the man was watching Robin closely again. His golden eyes blazed, and Robin suddenly got the eerie feeling that he was reading her thoughts. He raised his head and seemed to be listening to the wind outside. Robin thought she had never seen such a handsome young man, but she also wasn't sure she had ever met one quite as strange.

"Whoever kills this vampire must make certain that she is killed entirely. Not one strand of hair or even a thread of her clothing must remain."

"But if I . . . or, rather, someone kills her, will her . . . her victim recover?" Robin asked in a shaky voice.

"Indeed, your little brother will recover," the man said with a strange grin. "So far, no one has been brave enough to go after the vampire, except for . . ."

There was not one second of time to waste. First, Robin had to keep her promise to Harry to be home before dark. Then she had to figure out how to kill this wicked old vampire who lived on Diablo Mountain. Robin finished tying her left shoe and then pulled her backpack over her shoulder quickly.

"Wait!" the young man said in a sharp voice. "A cab will be here in 40 minutes, and the sun is setting soon. No young person is safe after dark!"

But Robin was already moving toward the door. "I have to get home!" she insisted. "There isn't much time."

"Then remember this," the man said as he followed her closely, laying a hand on Robin's shoulder. "There is more than one way to kill a vampire."

Robin just nodded, though she didn't really know what he meant. She broke into a quick run as soon as she was out the station door.

"And wait until the full moon!" the young man called after her. "Not tonight! Wait!"

Wait? Robin thought as the station disappeared behind her. *I can't wait at all!*

Now pink and deep orange glowed in the sky as the sun dipped behind the hills.

Faster, Robin said to herself. *Run faster!*

Minute by minute, the sky grew dimmer. Off toward the hills, Robin thought she heard an eerie howling. Was that just her imagination?

Sweat trickled down Robin's forehead, and her backpack banged against her back as she made the turn toward her home. *Only one more mile. Keep moving!*

As Robin turned down the street where her home was, the sun disappeared. The last glimmers of daylight were fading, and the first long fingers of darkness began creeping toward Robin. Just as her house came into view, Robin heard an odd leathery sound. It grew closer and closer . . .

"*UGH!*"

Robin yelled as a giant bat swooped right

in front of her face. It came so close that she could smell a damp, sickening odor as it beat its wings. Robin clasped her hands around her neck and dashed at race speed toward her house. But the bat was superfast. Leathery wings blinded her with flapping, and suddenly Robin felt the prickly claws of the bat gripping her on either side of her neck. Robin swatted at the bat frantically, but it would not let go. Now the bat's mouth was opening near Robin's neck. She could feel a trickle of something wet oozing out of the bat's mouth, and then the touch of razor-sharp teeth . . .

"Robin!"

Robin's father stepped out on the porch and turned on the bright porch light. Instantly, the bat flew away with a hiss. Breathlessly, Robin whirled around to watch the bat disappear down the dark road. She shuddered as she rubbed her neck. That light had come on just in time. One second longer and the bat—the *vampire*— would have had her teeth in Robin's neck.

Robin leaned against her dad and hugged him tightly. When she looked at him, she could tell he'd been crying.

"Was that you calling, sweetie?" her dad asked in an exhausted voice. "I'm so sorry we didn't answer, but both your mother and I were at Harry's bedside and . . ."

"Harry? Is he any better?" Robin interrupted, still trying to catch her breath.

Her father shook his head. "Hour by hour, he grows weaker. I don't know how much longer he has."

Robin glanced at her watch. It was a little after 8:00. *Not even 48 hours*, Robin thought desperately, but all she said was, "I have to see him."

When Robin walked to her brother's bedside, she tried to remain calm for Harry's sake, but it wasn't easy. Harry looked as though all the blood had been drained from his face. Sunken, pained eyes stared blankly at Robin. She wasn't sure Harry even recognized her. Harry tried to open his mouth to speak, but no words came out. His jaw just moved awkwardly from side to side. His breathing was ragged and shallow.

Gently, Robin pulled the blankets away from her brother's neck and leaned closer. Along a thick vein in Harry's neck were two distinct puncture marks. To the side of the punctures were slight scratches where it appeared that the vampire bat had grasped Harry's neck with its claws while it drank his blood. Robin took a deep breath. If she had been unsure whether or not this vampire was real, she wasn't any longer.

"It's okay, Harry," Robin said quietly as she stroked hair off his forehead. "I'm going to make sure you get better." Robin paused and then added, "I promise."

Much later that night, around 4 a.m., Robin crept out of bed. She had been awake all night figuring out the best way to put an end to the vampire. In movies and books, vampires were always killed by putting a stake or knife through their heart. That ought to work. But Robin realized that she'd have to surprise the vampire by catching her asleep wherever she was hiding on Diablo Mountain. That would be her only chance of overpowering the strengthened vampire.

Robin knew that the vampire would return to her hiding place just before dawn. Robin figured if she hid behind the trees, she could watch and follow behind the vampire and see where she was hiding. Then just after sunrise, when the vampire should be fast asleep, Robin would sneak in and drive the knife through the very heart of the hideous old monster. The thought of what she had to do made Robin shiver and feel sick to her stomach.

Robin was a little concerned that the vampire might still be in the form of a bat if she hadn't fed on a victim. And there would be no way Robin could follow a bat in the dim pre-dawn light. But she didn't have time to figure out another plan or worry about all the *what ifs?* It was time to take action and hope for the best.

Robin put on her darkest clothes and her fastest running shoes and tiptoed into the kitchen, where she grabbed the longest, sharpest knife she could find. Robin didn't even like to kill the flies that sometimes got into her dorm room, so she couldn't imagine where she'd find the bravery to put this knife through the heart of a vampire. *But I've got to find it*, she thought to herself. From the kitchen, she could hear Harry struggling to breathe in his room down the hall. *I will find it*, she concluded grimly.

With that, Robin slipped out the front door and into the moonlit night. Looking at the moon, she noticed it was nearly full, but not quite. It would be full tomorrow night. The words of the handsome man in the train station came back to her: "Wait until the full moon." Robin wondered why he had said that, but it didn't matter. She couldn't wait another 24 hours to save Harry's life. Robin worried that her little brother might not even make it through another day.

Now Robin began running down an old,

hidden path that led to the base of the mountain. The mountain appeared ghostly and dangerous in the glow of the setting moon. Robin listened closely for the sound of beating wings or footsteps, but the countryside was absolutely still. Finally, the path came out to the only road that led up to the mountaintop. Robin crouched behind a huge ancient oak tree and waited. If she had predicted correctly, the vampire should be coming along within the next half hour. In the distance, a dog barked. A low wind whistled through the trees. And then . . .

There she was!

A tall woman in a long black cape moved quickly along the road toward where Robin hid. As the vampire got closer, the same damp, dead scent that Robin had smelled on the bat drifted her way. And when the vampire passed by, Robin could see her sunken red eyes glowing in the dark and looking from one side of the road to the other. Suddenly, the vampire stopped. She cocked her head to one side, listening.

"Who's there?" she finally hissed in a low, evil voice. She turned her head, and her eyes glowed in Robin's direction.

Robin held her breath. She prayed that the vampire couldn't hear her heart pounding.

Screeeeee!

At that moment, a fat raccoon squealed as it ran past the vampire. And in a flash, the vampire grabbed the raccoon by the tail. Robin watched in horror as the vampire bared her sharp teeth in the moonlight and sunk them into the neck of the struggling raccoon. In seconds, the animal went limp. Long sucking sounds came from the vampire as she drank the raccoon's blood. Then she tossed the dead raccoon into the woods. Streaks of blood dripped from her mouth, and her eyes suddenly glowed more brightly.

Satisfied, the vampire continued moving along the road up the mountain. Robin kept a safe distance behind her, always remaining hidden in the trees. She hoped that the vampire was too tired and full to pay much attention to what was happening twenty yards back down the road. As Robin crept along, the moon was getting lower and lower, making it harder to see. But finally, the vampire turned off the road and climbed up a short path that led to a cave.

I knew it! Robin thought to herself.

Robin had suspected that the vampire was living in the cave. The Diablo Mountain cave was reported to be full of bats, some of them infected with rabies, so no one ever went near it. It was the perfect hiding place for the old monster. Robin watched her crouch down and then crawl quickly into the small dark opening. Robin looked at her watch. All she had to do now was wait until the sunrise in about twenty minutes. Robin was pretty certain that nothing could wake a vampire after sunrise once it was asleep in its hiding place. At least, that's the way it was in books and movies.

Driving that knife into her heart should be easy, then, Robin tried to assure herself. But her hands were already shaking. Going into a bat-filled cave was bad enough, but killing a vampire? It wouldn't be long now . . .

Suddenly the stillness was shattered by the sound of crunching stone and then a loud boom.

"Oh, no!" Robin whispered.

The vampire had rolled a huge boulder into the opening of the cave. Robin remembered what the young man in the station had said about the vampire being unnaturally strong after hunting. She knew right away that she would probably not be able to push that boulder back out of the way. Even so, Robin waited for the sunrise. As soon as the first rays spilled over the mountaintop, Robin rushed to the opening of the cave and put all her weight against the boulder. It was like trying to move a brick wall. Robin pounded her fists on the boulder. There was not even a hint of movement.

Robin slumped down against the boulder and put her face in her hands. "What am I going to do now?" she asked out loud through tears. If she couldn't kill the vampire tonight, Harry would die. *Think!* she said silently to herself. *This will be your last chance!*

Before Robin had gotten back home, she had come up with a new plan. It would be very dangerous and about as scary as she could imagine anything could be, but she couldn't think of any other way to kill the vampire.

For most of the day, Robin sat at Harry's bedside, dozing and watching her brother. His condition was slowly getting worse, and Robin was pretty sure that her brother no longer recognized her. Every ten minutes or so, her parents would come in and check on Harry. Part of Robin wanted to tell her parents about the vampire and ask them for help. But a larger part of her knew that her parents wouldn't believe her. Worse than that, they'd keep an eye on her and make sure she didn't leave the house if she started talking about going out to kill a vampire in the middle of the night. Then Harry would be lost.

"Hold on, buddy," Robin murmured to

her brother. "You're going to be all right. I promise."

She looked at her watch. Precious time was ticking away. But there was nothing she could do until after dark. "Come on, sunset," she whispered.

I'm inside the Diablo Hill cave. Move the boulder blocking the entrance. I'll explain everything when I get out.
                                        Robin

Robin wrote the note quickly and left it on the kitchen counter at 3 a.m. Then she grabbed the long knife again and a flashlight and slipped out the front door without a sound. The full moon gave Robin plenty of light for running back to the mountain along the hidden path. Again, she listened for the beating of leathery wings, but there was no sound.

The vampire must do most of her feeding earlier in the evening, Robin thought as she moved along. *I just need to be hidden in that cave before she gets there.*

Robin's plan made her sick with fear, but she was going ahead with it. It was the only way. She would have to hide inside the cave with all the bats and who knows what else until the vampire came back. Even worse,

Robin would have to remain hidden while the vampire rolled the boulder in place. Once trapped inside the cave, Robin would wait until the vampire went to sleep. And then she'd put an end to the vampire's life.

And then I'll be locked inside a cave full of bats and a dead vampire until someone comes to rescue me, Robin thought grimly.

WOOOOOOOOOOO!!

Suddenly, a terrible howling echoed across the valley. Robin jumped and ducked behind a tree. Robin had heard coyotes before, but this sounded like something much bigger and much fiercer. Did vampires howl? Robin picked up her pace toward the cave, looking behind her constantly. At one point, just below the cave, the sound of wings getting closer and closer terrified Robin. Then several bats passed close by. In the bluish moonlight, Robin watched them swoop into the cave.

Just regular, everyday gross bats, she reassured herself. Even so, she gripped the long knife more tightly as she approached the opening to the cave. Before stepping inside, Robin turned to look back down the mountain. In the distance, she could barely make out a tall, black figure moving swiftly up the mountain road. It was the vampire. Robin would have plenty of time to get well hidden, but seeing the vampire made her heart pound and her hands shake.

The inside of the cave smelled rotten, and the constant scurrying noise of bats overhead and in dark corners made Robin's skin crawl. Carefully, Robin turned on the flashlight. She almost wished she hadn't. At least two hundred bats hung from the ceiling, and the sudden light made them squeal and flap their bony wings and move away from her.

"Oh, man," Robin whispered with a shudder. She swept the flashlight around the small cave, and what she saw next made her blood chill.

Placed in the middle of the cave was a dusty black coffin. The lid was pried open, and the inside of the coffin was caked with black soil.

"The vampire's sleeping chamber," Robin murmured nervously. She stepped over and examined it more closely. A small pool of half-dried blood was smeared through the soil, and a musty dead smell drifted up from it. Hundreds of glistening maggots and worms threaded through the soil, making the entire inside of the coffin quiver. Robin backed away, feeling a little dizzy and sick. It was time to hide. The vampire would be back soon.

As Robin searched for the darkest corner to hide in, she heard more eerie howling off in the distance. It was too far away now to be the vampire. Whatever it was, it could not possibly be as dangerous as a killer vampire. Robin finally found a small space behind a large rock near the back of the cave. She turned off the flashlight and held her breath.

Crunch, crunch . . .

The vampire's footsteps approached the cave. Robin could see her outline in the full moon. As soon as the vampire entered the cave, the bats all flew down from the roof of the cave to greet her. There was a great deal of squeaking and beating of wings. Robin shivered in her hiding place. Then the largest bat hopped on the vampire's shoulder and seemed to be saying something in her ear. Suddenly, the vampire's red eyes burned a furious red.

"*What?*" she screeched as she looked wildly about the cave. "Who dares to hide in my cave? Prepare to be killed and drained of every drop of blood in your body!"

Robin froze. The vampire's eyes glowed directly at her. Now the vampire was moving toward Robin and cornering her. Bats flew at her, blinding her with their leathery wings.

"Oh! Help!" Robin shouted desperately. But she knew no one could help her far up on Diablo Mountain. In the split second before the vampire reached her, Robin turned on the bright flashlight. Instantly, the bats disappeared into dark corners, and the vampire shrunk back with a hiss.

It was the break Robin needed.

Robin tore out of the cave at race speed, gravel and dirt flying up behind her. Down the trail and out to the old road she sped, but the vampire was gaining on her. It seemed as though the faster Robin ran, the closer the vampire got to her. Every now and then, Robin would turn the flashlight backward toward the vampire. The vampire would growl and fall back a bit, but it wasn't enough.

She's too strong! I can't beat her, Robin thought in a panic. *She's going to catch me!*

"You can't escape me, you fool!" the vampire hissed with a hollow, deadly laugh. "Now I've got you! Ha!"

Robin felt a bony claw grip her shoulder painfully. In one motion, the vampire threw Robin to the ground. The flashlight flew out of Robin's hand and shattered against a rock. Robin gripped the knife and threatened the leering vampire with it, but a swift kick from the vampire sent the knife flying into some roadside bushes.

The vampire held Robin firmly to the ground and grinned a ghastly grin. In horror,

Robin saw the vampire's sharp fangs glowing in the light of the setting full moon.

"First your little brother, and now you," the vampire said as she bared her sharp fangs. "Stupid, little, pathetic fools!"

"Help me! *HELP!*" Robin screamed.

The vampire threw her head back and laughed in an evil shriek. "No one can hear you! Call for help as loudly as you want, but—"

Growwwl!

All Robin saw was a huge creature leap from the bushes. Howling and snarling, the creature ripped the vampire off Robin and began wrestling with her. The vampire hissed and spat on the creature, but she was not able to pin him down. Before the full moon fell behind the mountain, Robin got a good look at the creature.

"What is it?" Robin murmured as she backed away. He stood on hind legs like a man, but his arms and legs were muscular and covered in fur. A small torn jacket hung from his chest, and his face—Robin could hardly believe it—his face was a wolf's face.

Werewolf!

"Let me go!" the vampire screamed. The werewolf had finally managed to pull the vampire's arms behind her back in a lock. He panted with his tongue hanging out and his rows of sharp teeth gleaming. Now the werewolf looked at Robin and nodded. Then, in a strange, gravelly voice that sounded halfway like a bark, he said, "Good job. You ran just fast enough to make her chase you too far from her cave. Now, she's in trouble."

"No! Let me go, or else you'll both die!" the vampire sputtered weakly. She suddenly sounded afraid and defeated. Strength seemed to be draining from her by the second.

The werewolf pointed to the east. Out toward the valley, bands of red and pink rose in the sky.

Suddenly, the vampire broke free. Robin gasped and turned to run, but then a strange thing happened. Instead of going after Robin, the vampire turned in the other direction, making a crazed dash up the road toward her cave.

"Now watch," the werewolf growled. His eyes met Robin's, and Robin thought the werewolf was smiling . . . if it was even possible for a werewolf to smile.

The vampire had not run more than fifty yards when the first rays of sunlight shot across the valley and onto the mountain. The very moment the sun touched her shoulder, the vampire collapsed lifeless on the mountain road. A puff of smoke rose from her mouth, and then she burst into flames.

"So, you see, there's more than one way to kill a vampire," the werewolf said with a cough, and then he groaned.

Robin turned to look at him. As soon as the sun hit him, he fell panting and squirming on the ground. The werewolf appeared to be in extreme pain. His face and body were changing rapidly, magically. His long wolf snout shrank, and the fur on his face, arms, and legs simply disappeared. His huge wolf body shriveled down to half its size, and suddenly the tattered coat fit him. The creature rolled over to look at Robin, but he was no longer a creature . . .

He was the young man from the train station!

"It's . . . it's you!" Robin said in amazement. "But I don't understand. How . . . ?"

The man struggled to speak. "Every full moon I hunt vampires wherever they cause trouble. I've been trying to kill this vampire for months, but I've needed help. She was just too strong. Because you brought her so far away from her cave this close to sunrise, I was able to overpower her."

Robin just stared at him as he continued to transform. He seemed to be in agony. Then, all of a sudden, the man jumped up and staggered in the direction of the flaming vampire.

"Quickly!" he shouted hoarsely. "Don't let

any bit of the vampire's soul escape! Even the smallest shred can turn back into the vampire!"

Crawling, slithering, and squirming away from the vampire's burning body were lizards, snakes, and worms.

"Capture them all and throw them back in the flames," the young man gasped as he fell back to the ground again. "Don't let any escape!"

Robin rushed toward the flames. Although it made her skin crawl, she grasped all the lizards and worms quickly and threw them in the fire. They made popping and sizzling noises as they burned. The snakes were harder and scarier to catch. Although they were small, they had the same red eyes as the vampire, and they hissed like the vampire when Robin picked them up. One even bared its small sharp fangs and lunged toward Robin's neck, but at the last second, she flung the snake into the flames.

Finally, every remnant of the vampire was burned down to a small pile of greenish ash. Robin even ground the ashes into the dirt to make absolutely certain that nothing remained. Then she turned to give a thumbs-up sign to the mysterious young man, but to her surprise, he was nowhere in sight. He had disappeared as quickly as he had appeared just before dawn. But Robin didn't spend any time looking for the young man or wondering what had happened to him. She had only one thought on her mind.

Robin raced home as quickly as she had run away from the vampire. Would Harry really be okay? When she reached the house, Robin slipped in the front door very quietly. It was still quite early, and she didn't want to startle anyone. She tiptoed toward the kitchen and . . .

"Robin! Hey!"

There sat Harry at the kitchen table, his mouth full of Froot Loops, a surprised grin on his face. Robin rushed to her brother and put her arms around him.

"You're okay!" she said in a choked voice. "You look completely better."

Harry just nodded and grabbed another handful of Froot Loops right out of the box.

"I had a funny dream about a wolf chasing a bat right before I woke up," Harry said with a shrug. "When I woke up, it was still dark, and I still felt really bad. Then, as soon as the sun came up, I felt as good as new. And hungry!"

Robin smiled and breathed a long sigh of relief. Then she remembered the note she had left on the kitchen counter. She carefully picked it up and put it in her pocket. No one would need to know what had happened.

Harry might believe her, but her parents never would.

"How come you look so messy?" Harry suddenly asked, eyeing her dusty shoes and crazy hair. "What have you been doing?"

Robin grinned as she sat down across from Harry and grabbed some Froot Loops.

"Just been out running as fast as I could," Robin said. "And keeping a promise to someone important to me."

The next day, Robin had her parents drive her to the train station earlier than she really needed to be there. She wanted to talk to the young man behind the ticket counter about the vampire and what it was like being a werewolf. Everything was beginning to seem as if it had just been some kind of wild dream. Had it really even happened? In spite of herself, Robin was beginning to have some doubts.

But to Robin's disappointment, a woman was working the ticket counter.

"Excuse me," Robin said to her, "but do you know when the young man with the long hair might be working?"

"You're out of luck," the woman said with a wink. "Ben just transferred to the Springfield station today."

"His name is Ben?" Robin asked. "Do you know why he left?"

Now the woman gave Robin a strange look and just shrugged. "Said he had something he had to do in Springfield. That's all I know."

Robin sighed and sat down to wait for her train. Springfield was 200 miles in the opposite direction. *Why would he suddenly transfer there?* Robin wondered. She stared out the window at Diablo Mountain in the distance. Had it all been a dream or some kind of weird illusion? Was she losing her mind?

Robin picked up a newspaper and began leafing through it, not really paying much attention to the articles. Suddenly, however, a headline jumped out at her and made her catch her breath: *Another Springfield Child Suffers from Mysterious Bite: Doctors Baffled*.

Robin looked back out the window toward the mountains to the south and murmured, "Good luck, Ben."

■ ■ ■